Dear Parent:
Your child's love of reading starts here!

Every child learns to read in a different way and at his or her own speed. Some go back and forth between reading levels and read favorite books again and again. Others read through each level in order. You can help your young reader improve and become more confident by encouraging his or her own interests and abilities. From books your child reads with you to the first books he or she reads alone, there are I Can Read Books for every stage of reading:

SHARED READING

Basic language, word repetition, and whimsical illustrations, ideal for sharing with your emergent reader

BEGINNING READING

Short sentences, familiar words, and simple concepts for children eager to read on their own

READING WITH HELP

Engaging stories, longer sentences, and language play for developing readers

READING ALONE

Complex plots, challenging vocabulary, and high-interest topics for the independent reader

ADVANCED READING

Short paragraphs, chapters, and exciting themes for the perfect bridge to chapter books

I Can Read Books have introduced children to the joy of reading since 1957. Featuring award-winning authors and illustrators and a fabulous cast of beloved characters, I Can Read Books set the standard for beginning readers.

A lifetime of discovery begins with the magical words **"I Can Read!"**

Visit www.icanread.com for information
on enriching your child's reading experience.

JUST A
BABY BIRD

BY MERCER MAYER

HARPER

An Imprint of HarperCollinsPublishers

To Emma and Lily
Scheckner

I Can Read Book® is a trademark of HarperCollins Publishers.

Library of Congress Control Number: 2015948299
ISBN 978-0-06-226535-7 (trade bdg.) — ISBN 978-0-06-147821-5 (pbk.)
15 16 17 18 19 SCP 10 9 8 7 6 5 4 3 2 1 ❖ First Edition

A Big Tuna Trading Company, LLC/J. R. Sansevere Book
www.littlecritter.com

Little Sister and I play
in the yard.

We hear "Peep, peep, peep."

We find a baby bird.

But where is the momma bird?

We look. Dad helps.

We do not find the momma bird.

We tiptoe to the baby bird.

We are so very careful.

But the baby bird hops away.

Dad pokes holes in a box.

He carefully catches the baby
bird with the box.
"Let's find the nest," says Dad.

We look high in the trees.

We look low in the bushes.

We look everywhere.

We do not find a nest,
but Dad gets stuck in a tree.

15

We make a little nest.
If the momma bird is near,
she will feed her baby.

We hide and wait.

The baby bird peeps and peeps.

No momma bird comes.

The baby bird must be hungry.
Mom searches online
to find the right food.

Mom makes dinner for the
baby bird.
Our bird loves it.

We make a bed for the baby
bird in an old fish tank.
He is safe.

Dad puts a towel over the tank.

Now the baby bird will sleep.

We say, "Good night, Baby Bird."

Day after day the baby bird grows bigger and bigger. Our baby bird is so big.

Dad says, "Baby Bird is too big.

I built a birdhouse.

Maybe our bird will stay."

We open the tank outside.
Our baby bird flies away.
"Where will he go?" I ask.

"Some birds fly south
for the winter," says Mom.
"Maybe our bird will be back."

Summer ends.

Fall ends, too.

Winter comes. I always look
for our bird.

Spring is here.

I hear "Tweet, tweet, tweet."

We all run to see.

Our bird sits on the birdhouse.

He is much bigger now.

"Look!" I say.

"Our bird has a family, too.

How cool is that?"

He was just a baby bird.
Now he is grown up—
with a baby bird of his own!